KU-345-336

Last

of the

Leatherbacks

Last of the
Leatherbacks

D. J. BRAZIER

with illustrations by
Wendy Murray

Matador
9 De Montfort Mews
Leicester LE1 7FW, UK
Tel: (+44) 116 255 9311 / 9312
Email: books@troubador.co.uk
Web: www.troubador.co.uk/matador

ISBN 978-1905237-692

Typeset in 12pt Myriad by Troubador Publishing Ltd, Leicester, UK
Printed in the UK by The Cromwell Press Ltd, Trowbridge, Wilts, UK

Matador is an imprint of Troubador Publishing Ltd

For Debbie

Contents

Part One

The Hatching

A final lunge and she broke through.

With her head suddenly clear of the suffocating sand the baby turtle gulped the cool night air. Waves of oxygen rippled through her, tingling the tips of her numb flippers as she pulled her aching body up and onto the beach. For three long nights she had fought her way up from the egg chamber a metre below, and now as she lay gathering her strength, the ground gave way beneath her and dozens of her siblings broke surface in an eruption of sand and flailing flippers.

Within moments a heaving, struggling mass of sixty hatchlings had engulfed her, all slapping and kicking each other in their frantic haste to escape the nest. Two or three clambered across her and shoved her back into the bale of tumbling turtles, and she spread her flippers and kicked hard with her rear paddles, and managed to scramble out onto a patch of firm sand. Another hatchling barged into her, butting her cheek, and then another slapped her face, and each slap transmitted a contagious shock of stimulation, an irresistible demand to join the stampede.

The baby turtle flicked out her fore flippers, pulled hard, and shot forward a full body length, so ignorant of her own strength that she ploughed head first into a sand furrow. She pulled herself free and squinted at the charge of baby turtles all around her; blurred bodies disappearing from view, dropping into sand gullies or stumbling into tussocks of incense grass, all heading to where the moon's reflection on breaking waves painted the sky a shimmering silver in the distance.

She raised herself again, spread her flippers and flicked forward, driven by an instinct which gave only one command – reach the sea. She could hear the sea, and smell it, and deep in ancestral memory she could see it, and taste it. The baby turtle had no idea how far away it was, she knew only that the sea was life.

The fox stood with head cocked and his charcoal-tipped ears twitching in the chill night air. The clacking call he had heard earlier now bounced towards him, and a flash of white wing ripped through the dune's shadow as a nightjar clapped by, mouth agape from ear to ear, trawling insects.

The fox leapt and snapped at the fat bird, and missed, and landed with one paw buried in a tangle of goat creeper vines. Three beetles scrambled out of the vines and fled towards the gloom clinging to the dune's base, and the fox bounded after them, and crunched and swallowed them one by one.

A gust of wind hissed through the marram grass and the fox padded to the top of the dune to taste the breeze, and inhaled the heavy fragrance of oleander blooms unfurling to tempt the first insects of dawn.

Bird chatter rattled out from the palm trees and an

unkindness of ravens raked the sky above, heading for the fishing village five miles away, where fishermen would soon be spreading their catches of sardines to dry in the sun before pounding them into cattle feed and fertiliser.

The fox turned his head and listened to the muffled boom of breakers on the coral reef. He knew the high tide would soon ebb and he would have to hurry if he was to scour the strandline and reach his den before sunrise.

Another gust of wind stroked his fur and the fox sniffed, then inhaled again, longer this time, his amber eyes glinting as he tried to identify a faint scent carried on the breeze. Then in two bounds he descended the dune and loped off towards the sea.

The baby turtle now clambered through a patch of sticky leaves and the rancid tang of decaying seed pods filled her nostrils, overpowering the salt promise of the sea. Suddenly a huge spider scurried across her path, raised its jaws and challenged her, its long barbed legs trembling as it gathered information. Then it lunged forward, plucked a caterpillar from a seed pod beside the turtle, and marched off towards the palm trees.

The baby turtle flung herself clear of the vegetation and entered a wide swath of sand hills notched with the trails of the night hunters – scorpions, spiders and geckos, all hurrying to reach the safety of their shady crevices and burrows before dawn. Her flippers sank and dragged through this fine, soft sand and each lunge and pull seemed to demand more strength than the last.

She climbed a towering hill and paused at the top, heart pounding, and she could just make out the bump shapes of three of her siblings heading toward's the hill's seaward slope.

Then a series of rapid thumps approached from behind, sending tremors through her plastron. A long tufted tail whipped over her head and a pair of elongated feet flicked salt powder in her face as a jerboa touched down and immediately sprang away. Then an excited, high pitched bark lanced the air and the baby turtle launched herself towards the hill's crest.

The fox pounced. His forepaws came together on the turtle's back, pinning her down, punching the air from her lungs and pushing her into the sand. One front flipper twisted painfully beneath her and a sharp spasm of pain tore through her neck as her head was forced up and backwards. Then the weight lifted as the fox spun to his left, and bounded towards another hatchling. The baby turtle flapped her fore flippers and pushed hard with her rear paddles, and moved to within a body length of the hill's crest. Her flippers stretched and swept through the air as she tottered on the brink, then two thumps shook her rear paddles and she toppled over the edge.

The next moment hot damp breath slopped along the turtle's back and sharp teeth scraped across her head. Then a fang pierced the soft pink patch on her skull and her mouth sprang open. A furred tongue bulged into her mouth, and her sharp-ridged jaws snapped shut.

The fox's head jerked up, with the baby turtle hanging from his tongue tip. He sat back on his haunches and swiped at the hatchling with both forelegs, clawing the air, then he whipped his head from side to side until he broke the baby turtle's bite and she tumbled down the hill's flank, and came to a halt in a midden of seed pods piled up in the entrance to a crab plover's burrow.

Angry yaps came from the hill's summit as the baby turtle thrust her flippers into the sand and flicked forward into the dark burrow, scrambling over seed pods and crab shells.

The fox lowered his head and padded down the hill, snuffling the baby turtle's tracks. Halfway down he stopped, and sniffed at a whiff of hatchling scent wafting out from a crab plover burrow. He thrust his snout into the hole, ploughing through crab shells and guano, and a feather nib pricked his nose and he leapt backwards, his sudden movement pinching the quill against the burrow's ceiling and bending it into his mouth, where the shaft sprang open and hooked the blood blister left by the baby turtle's bite. Yelping with pain the fox pawed frantically at the feather now snagged in his teeth until it flew clear of his mouth, ripping the blister as it did so.

The fox sat and licked the long tufts of hair covering the underside of his paw, trying to wipe the sting from his swelling tongue. His stomach gurgled and he glanced towards the honeycombed rocks at the base of the cliffs, where the lizards lived. But he knew that the feral dogs who killed his mother could soon be scouring the beach so he turned and loped away, choosing a route through the highest sand hills, where ranks of darkling beetles held the crests, their carapaces gleaming with beads of fog gleaned moisture.

The baby turtle clambered out of the burrow, butting a fox blood stalactite. Her baggy throat sack pulsated with shallow pants as she scanned the sky for a lunar glow now bleached by anaemic light. Then a slight gust of sea breeze stroked her face and her senses realigned to the draw of her ocean home. She flicked forward, heading for the soft hued curves of the sand drifts and beyond, to where a slack tide had turned to ebb, and a reef-sieved lagoon had begun to empty.

The Race to the Sea

The baby turtle swept and kicked her way across the shells and seaweed humps of the strandline, oblivious to the shrill cries of seabirds descending to harvest the rich bounty deposited by the high tide.

She clambered up and over a tangle of oyster thief weed, and peered at the expanse of tidal plain stretching before her. To her water-destined eyes the rippled plain seemed to sway and swirl in a blur of birds and turtle hatchlings. Closest to her, strutting oyster catchers plundered the strandline, their brilliant red beaks probing for sand lice, while beyond them the bright orange legs of sandpipers pranced across her vision, their brown mottled bodies held close to the ground and their grey heads bobbing as they searched for sandhoppers and seaslaters. Further away, mobs of redshanks bustled back and forth across the plain, flicking over mitre and bonnet shells,

14

seeking moon snails and hermit crabs.

And between the redshanks and the receding sea, a column of exhausted baby turtles flippered into a gauntlet of ghost crabs.

The leading hatchling was no more than a few metres from the sea when the first crab struck. Seizing the turtle's flippers in both pincers the crab compressed his claws, snipping tendons and crippling his prey. The hatchling rocked from side to side, spasms twitching her flippers as the crab dragged her to the edge of its burrow and scuttled away to intercept another victim.

As if this initial strike had been a signal to commence the attack, the plain now teemed with scores of stalk-eyed scavengers. Defenceless against the crabs' speed and snapping claws the hatchlings were decimated.

The larger crabs performed their butchery with a terrible efficiency, severing flippers or decapitating their victims with a single pinch. Hatchlings caught in smaller claws were merely immobilised so their assailants could begin to feed, tearing off chunks of tender flesh for four pairs of jaws to chew and cram into a grinding gastric mill. Only when weight of turtle numbers overwhelmed a solitary crab, or when a hatchling was seized in immature claws did any manage to break free and scramble towards the sea.

And with the copper red sun now climbing above the bay, more and more daylight predators converged to share the spoils – fan-tailed ravens and black-backed gulls now combed the pale sky above the plain, screeching and jostling for position before plunging down to snatch any survivors of the ghost crab slaughter.

The baby turtle reached the seaward edge of the strandline, and swept her front flippers to pull herself clear, but a strand of oyster thief weed had wrapped around her left paddle and held her firm. She spread her flippers and tugged her trapped paddle but the seaweed strap restraining her had been cured in saltwater and remained strong, and elastic. She twisted her head, trying to bite the thing which held her, then pushed hard against the seaweed's pebble anchor. But the damp snare held fast, and drew tighter with every effort she made. A brittle star exposed by her struggles cringed away from the sunlight, and then a pair of scarlet capped stalk-eyes, cloudy and unblinking, rose clear of the sand a few inches to her left.

The stalk-eyes keeled over and disappeared. Three stiletto-tipped legs curled up onto the beach, and the old crab's pale body pitched out of his burrow.

The senescent scavenger paused for just a moment, tasting the air, then he scuttled towards the hatchling.

A searing pain shot through the baby turtle's right flipper as the crab closed his claw, puncturing her flesh. She tried to pull her flipper free from the pincers' grasp, but the crab tightened his grip, pinching her tendon. She pushed down and pulled with both flippers and rear paddles, but the crab simply

clenched his legs and wrenched harder, and stretched his second claw to grab her other flipper. Tiny studs of seawater squeezed from the seaweed restraining the hatchling, then the edge of a razorfish shell cut the strap and it ripped, and the baby turtle toppled forward.

Grains of sand clogged the hatchling's mouth as the crab tugged her clear and dragged her to the edge of his burrow. The crab hooked two legs inside the burrow's mouth and the baby turtle felt her body lift and tilt as the crab began to haul her downwards. She slapped her left flipper against the burrow's rim, demolishing the edge, and the crab grasped her flipper's tip in his other claw and pinched so hard that fibres in her tendon tore and a trickle of blood oozed from the puncture wound.

But the turtle could now hear the sea, and smell it, and she dug her paddles into the sand and pulled as hard as she could, until the crab's opaque eyes blushed pink and yellow spit foamed from his mandibles. Then one of his legs twitched and shifted up the burrow wall and a second one trembled and began to straighten. The crab re-anchored his legs and pulled, but his joints were enfeebled by age and lack of nourishment, and he had not expected such determined resistance from his prey.

The turtle felt the crab's grip loosen and she pulled with all her remaining strength until a bubbling hiss leaked from the crab's gill chamber and a shiver ran through his claws, and suddenly one sprang open.

With her left flipper free the hatchling immediately flailed at the crab's eyes until he released her other flipper and dropped down into his burrow.

The baby turtle lay still for a moment, gulping sea air. Gnats jigged above her and a raven swaggered across her line of sight, stalking a hatchling-dragging crab. The crab reached its burrow and the raven cawed, and the crab flung its claws wide to confront this threat to its prize. Then while the raven hopped and skipped to hold the crab's attention, her mate snatched the dead hatchling and lifted away, flared wing-fingers kneading balls of air and sunlight glinting off his metallic black plumage.

The baby turtle flippered towards the sea, pushing her aching body past small pyramids of sand excavated by the ghost crabs. One juvenile crab clicked round to follow her progress, but the rest were preoccupied with protecting their spoils from gulls

and ravens, or masticating sand to seal their burrows against the rising sun.

The baby turtle reached the edge of the sea. Wet sand pressed against her plastron and a foam fringed wave swept towards her. Mouth agape, she raised her head and pushed down with both flippers as the wave's sizzling spume swept over her, shocking her hot body with a slap of cold water. She gulped, and tasted seawater. She flippered forward, her stupor flushed away, and sliced through sand-churning slosh, flicking and thrusting, until the next wave embraced her, and lifted her, and pushed her back up the beach. She lunged forward again, flapping across shell-studded ripples, while the spent wave sagged and gurgled behind her, then rumbled back down the slope and engulfed her, and carried her.

Bouyed by the denseness of seawater she surfed the silk sheet flow, abandoning her awkward paddling motion for butterfly strokes and rear-paddle kicks. She felt the tug of the undertow and responded with short, sharp strokes, slicing the water, until the sandy floor sloped away and she adopted a position just below the sea's crinkled surface, swimming with a smooth undulating motion, flipper tips coming together beneath her plastron and each stroke slightly more effective than the last.

She broke surface, snatched a lungful of air and swooped down again, and felt the pulse of the ebbing tide emptying the lagoon. One of her siblings swept by above, and she adjusted her paddle tilt and followed, blending her motion with the flow of the tidal river pouring out through the gap in the reef. The teardrop body of another hatchling appeared below, flippers sweeping and pumping, and her white dorsal lines glowing in the sunlight. All were racing against time and tide, pushing themselves past exhaustion to reach the safety of the deep water beyond the coral wall.

The baby turtle banked and swept into the main channel, where less than a metre of fast flowing water now covered the rock-ribbed bed, decreasing to half this depth where domes of brain coral bulged up towards the surface.

A silver-green shape cruised past on her left, and a sudden surge in the current shoved her downwards, skimming her across the horns of limestone saddles. Another sleek body arrowed past and in the next instant a silver bolt slammed into a hatchling directly

above her, sending the stunned creature reeling down towards her. Then a solid head flashed silver. Fang-lined jaws seized the hatchling and spurts of dark green blood stained the water. A tail fin whipped ahead. A stuttering pressure wave cuffed the baby turtle, and in a swirl of silver glints her sibling vanished.

The baby turtle kicked and swept, and swerved to avoid a flipperless hatchling spinning in the current. The crippled hatchling twirled and rose, streaming blood, too drained to hold her body below water any longer. She bobbed on the surface for only an instant before a pair of pink webbed feet sculled towards her and a hooked yellow beak closed around her head.

Another brain coral crowded the channel and the baby turtle rose and arced over the dome and immediately dropped into a shadow cast by a dense shoal of thousands of silver-blue fish, each no more than three inches long, packing the trough and blocking the hatchlings only escape route to the open sea.

The baby turtle swam along the rippling sardine wall to the rim of the channel and stopped, unwilling to leave the reassuring pull of the tidal river. She broke surface to snatch a breath and as she did so one of her siblings rose over the trough's rim and sped away, immediately pursued by a lurking kingfish.

Back in the channel's centre turtle hatchlings continued to circle and collide, and glance off the sardine shoal, while in the cloudless sky above a great white heron dropped towards the reef and a squabble of screaming gulls dropped with him.

The heron alighted on a bleached coral antler and began to fold his wings, but as he did so a pair of brawling black-backed gulls swooped past his face and he jumped, heavy wing beats shredding the air. Startled and off-balance he misjudged his take off and one dangling foot caught in a coral crown and snapped an antler, sending a pulsing crack of sound through the sardine shoal.

The shoal buckled, and split. Dozens of fish bolted and the flashes of bright silver as they fled were irresistible to the prowling barracuda. Some sped after the fleeing sardines while a phalanx of nine sennets struck the shoal, cleaving it apart in a slashing charge. The water boiled as batteries of barracuda tore into the sardines, heads snapping from side to side and bodies rolling as sharp teeth ripped chunks from their prey. Some sardines leapt clear of the water to escape the slashing teeth of the predators, and landed in the top forks of the coral branches; easy pickings for the heron who lunged and croaked with delight, his sword beak flashing silver with the scales of lanced sardines.

Aroused by the commotion the gulls and ravens now plunged into the shoal, plummeting down to pluck stunned and wounded fish from the surface.

And under such a furious assault the shoal disintegrated, clearing the channel, and the baby turtle raced through the gap in the coral reef, thrashing up spray as she left the beach and lagoon behind, and entered the welcoming swell of the open sea.

Part Two

The Ocean

The turtle moved to the edge of the table coral, flexed her flippers, and stretched them high above her. With one angled stroke she cleared the overhang and entered the shallows, where the fresh light of dawn was cleansing shadow-stains and brushing corals with soft colours.

She broke surface. Sky pale blue and cloudless. Moon more texture than light. Three porpoises breached and sighed a few metres away, and a shear-water sliced through the orange glow tingeing the horizon. The leatherback breathed deeply, flushing out stale lungs with refreshing cool air, and then she fanned her flippers and gurgled seawater as a squadron of eagle rays glided by beneath her.

Eleven years had passed since she escaped from the lagoon and clambered aboard a seaweed raft, the thick mat of tangled fronds providing shelter from winged and finned predators, and sustenance from jelly polyps and flying fish eggs. And for the next few months she went wherever the currents carried her, until one night when a water spout tore her raft apart, and the turtle's life of pelagic solitude began.

She spent her prepubescent years following vast smacks of jellyfish drifting with the currents, only occassionally encountering another of her kind; always much older than her, and always a female.

And now she lived by the time-rhythms of the open ocean – long days swimming through a void of blue, without sight of the seabed or a shoreline, and starlit nights spent cradled by surface swell, with her long wing flippers tucked safely beside her.

Sometimes when floating across a deep water shelf she could sense the presence of huge sharks, slipping silently up from the darkness, scything through schools of squid and fish. And sometimes she saw giant phosphorescent jellyfish rise, their viridian bells at least twelve metres across, and their tentacles drift-snaring slumbering creatures before they sank back into blackness, heavy with a crop of paralysed victims.

But now, with a carapace more than four feet long and swift propulsion provided by powerful front flippers, the only constant threats to the leatherback's life were large sharks, and orcas, and Man.

She dived and split a sphere of yellow tang peeling away from the sun and pouring into the dullness of their cave retreat where they would pass the sunlit hours squeezed amongst bigeyes and squirrelfish.

She sank with them and hung above the sea bed for a moment, then slowly pivoted to the East, aligning herself with pointers buried deep in the rocks below, plotting her course to the seamount where she had tasted the scent of a male leatherback turtle two years ago, the year before she attained sexual maturity. Before she felt this need to reproduce.

A sea snake ribboned across her line of sight and she checked her bearings once more, then stretched and carved her flippers in a sweeping powerstroke and resumed her journey; heading out across the breadth of the Indian Ocean towards Malaysia, and beyond; to Borneo, and the island of Sipadan.

Dolphins

Early morning. Calm sea. Crestless, long and unhurried mid-ocean waves, rolling along. The turtle yawned and dipped her head, and heard the sharp clicks of a dolphin scanning the water hundreds of metres away. An accompanying scanner on the dolphin's left flank echoed the clicks and moved closer to intercept the path of his companion, to concentrate their search-scope.

Suddenly the calls intensified, in volume and pitch. Evenly spaced clicks now merged to create a whirring, mewing sound, stroking the water, probing and confirming with sound and touch, massaging the turtle's body.

A third dolphin arrowed in from the turtle's right, with sparkling pennants of bubbles spinning from his tail flukes. A white belly flashed past the turtle as the dolphin shot from the water and crashed back down, slapping his broad tail flukes on the surface and dropping towards her in a punch of foam. The dolphin spun to horizontal and raced away, barking with excitement. The dolphin scouts had found the vast shoal of Indian mackerel, tens of metres deep and hundreds of metres in diameter – the turtle's humming shield from attack from below.

The turtle raised her head to breathe. A swell lifted her and she could see a white scar of foam to the West – breakers on a reef where there was no reef. The two thousand strong herd of spinner dolphins had heard their scouts excited calls and were now surging towards the turtle with astonishing speed, outstripping the seabirds stacked above them.

The turtle inhaled and sank ten feet, now fully alert. The noise of the approaching herd rumbled across her, preceded by a crescendo of clicks, squeaks and barks which sent waves of alarm through the mackerel shoal swaying beneath her.

In a roar of sound the lead dolphins appeared. Eighty-plus bulleting bodies swept above and below the turtle in four synchronised layers. The first and third layer wheeled away to her right, the second and fourth to her left – pincer attack.

Moments later the main pod arrived, tapered in front, bunched together, but now peeling open, with flashing bodies banking left and right, high and low, encircling the mackerel.

By now the noise was deafening; slams of sound from above and volleys of rapid fire crack-shots from below, shaking the turtle's entire body. Those dolphins which had dived beneath the mackerel now spiralled upwards, coiling around each other and lifting the fish towards the surface. Simultaneously the dolphin pincers closed, and the flanking dolphins shortened each pass, squeezing the mackerel into a compact ball. More dolphins streamed in to plug gaps in the carousel and the turtle could no longer separate individual dolphins from the water as sunlight bounced off their dappled hides. And the faster they swam the more astonishing became the illusion, until attainment of a certain speed granted near-invisibility.

The snare of sound tightened around the spinning shoal. A few fish bolted from the sides, but the dolphins held their positions while the deserters were quickly snapped up by yellowfin tuna.

Suddenly the signal came, and scores of dolphins tore into the baitball from all directions. Their schoolmates in the carousel held firm, shepherding the shoal, knowing their turn would come.

The attack intensified, and panicked mackerel butted the turtle's stomach as she swept towards the surface, cutting through bubble-plumes and whirlpools while dozens of dolphins shot past.

She surfaced, and gulped air. Dolphins leapt and fell all around her, some breaching and crashing down on their backs or bellies, while others slapped the surface with tail flukes for extra effect – pistol shots of sound which compressed the mackerel into an ever tighter ball. A few feet in front of her a pair of grey tail flukes split the slope of a wave, flinging an eight inch mackerel twenty feet in the air. The fish slammed down on the surface, stunned, then vanished in a swirl of water and a toothed beak. Another fish careened into the turtle's face, flapping around in a circle on its side, sound-crippled, its swim bladder ruptured.

The sea now had two surfaces – one quicksilver, boiling two feet above the blue. Grey dolphin fins sliced through the blue while flashing yellowfin tuna lanced through both, some punching into clear air in pursuit of their prey.

A bird storm swirled above, darkening the sky.

Many hundreds of black noddies and shearwaters hailed down, pelting through fish and water. Sooty terns whirled together in tornado-like funnels, some over eager birds colliding as they swerved through the mass of slashing wings and attempted to target individual fish, while the heavier gulls hovered and screamed, and plummeted down to take advantage of other birds' efforts.

A screeching, stabbing blanket of beaks smothered the leaping mackerel, and the ferocity of the avian attack bludgeoned the top layers of fish back beneath the surface, forcing the shoal downwards.

The turtle angled her flippers and dropped twenty feet. Bubble-spears drilled all around her, spear tips breaking as the birds unwrapped and plunged past, beaks agape and webbed feet thrusting. Tuna sped everywhere, twisting and darting, and a ten foot marlin flashed silver-blue, his sword beak slashing, then he blushed into black, whipped round and flashed brilliant blue again before departing as suddenly as he had arrived.

The scope and magnitude of the dolphins' attack now eased considerably, their click barrage decelerating as they allowed the shoal to sink away from aerial competition. Now the clashing of teeth and the cracking of fish bones were the dominant sounds, while from above came the muted thumps of birds still pelting the surface, their speed and weight carrying them to their targets.

For more than an hour the baitball was plundered. Herder dolphins swopped places with feeders, and shepherded the shoal to the surface, then allowed it to sink, many times, until all the herd were fed. By the time the surviving mackerel were allowed to regroup and drop into deeper water the shoal had been decimated by two-thirds.

The turtle rose through water clouded with fish oil. She surfaced, upending a dozing gull which aimed a blow at her head, then screeched its indignation and paddled away. Satiated shearwaters bobbed in the swell, free of the waterlogging threat which hobbled the departing terns and denied them rest at sea. Scores of dolphins leapt all around, individually, or in twos and threes, some content with an arcing porpoise leap while others somersaulted, and flipped themselves lengthways, or cartwheeled over a companion.

Others floated quietly, or passed comment on their comrades antics with a chattering remark, or a jaw-clap, or a complimentary tail slap. A few stood on their heads and wagged their tails in the air, while the more energetic ones held their bodies vertical and skipped across the waves. And every few seconds or so a gleaming dolphin missile exploded from the water and span through the horizontal or vertical axis as many as a dozen times before smacking down in a burst of spray.

The turtle inhaled and dropped, and headed away from the cetacean celebration, acutely aware of the hunger pangs cramping her stomach.

Ten minutes later she reached the edge of the dolphin herd and immediately spied a comb jelly pulsing with red and yellow lights. She moved towards it and a slow buzzing sound came from her right, then a whistle, and an excited chirp as a dolphin calf acoustically scanned her solidness, tracing shapes and contours. The turtle felt the purr-massage in her empty stomach most, and the other hollow parts of her body where the probing clicks penetrated through flesh and expanded again, ricocheting and reporting size and textures.

The calf whistled again, in a crisper, higher tone, and the next moment his sunlight marbled face appeared in front of the turtle, inquisitive black eye sparkling, and mouth held laughing-open. The turtle held the dolphin's stare while a torrent of chuckling chirps and squeaks poured forth, accompanied by a stream of bubbles. And then the young spinner nodded four or five times, and twirled and shot away.

The calf covered forty metres in an instant, then braked to a juddering halt and snapped round, and charged back towards the turtle. At the last moment he dived beneath her and flipped onto his back and fired a volley of clicks along the length of her body. Then he wiggled in front of her before darting off to her left, and encircling her in a porcelain glowing hoop. Next he zigzagged back and forth in front of her, bending and extending his body before suddenly twisting away - the flickering comb jelly had caught his attention.

The calf trapped the comb jelly between flipper and body, and carried it to the surface. He released it and

moved to one side, and then rolled beneath it and bounced, tail-tossing his new toy ten feet in the air. The comb jelly span and collapsed into itself, and slapped back in to the sea. The stunned, deflated mass had barely sunk below the surface before the calf moved in again and touched his lower jaw to the opaque lump and rolled it like a punctured ball along the length of his body, and tail-tossed it skywards once more.

The turtle rose to seize the comb jelly, food was scarce in this part of the ocean, and her hunger cramps were becoming more painful. The calf glanced down at her and barked, arching his back, and with his head and flukes held down he jaw-clapped a challenge. The turtle continued to rise and the calf flexed his body up and down, fins churning the water, and tail whipping until all the turtle could see was a blurred ball of bubbles. Then he popped out of his bubble cloud and dived beneath her and pumped his tail so fast that she was still facing downwards when he burst through the surface and slammed down directly above her, with a crack that made her head ache, and showering her with more bubbles.

As the bubbles cleared the calf's mother arrived, sweeping in from the turtle's left with a graceful, relaxed motion. She called to her cavorting offspring with a high toned signature whistle and the calf span round and darted towards her, bombarding her with delighted squeaks and chirps, turtle and jelly forgotten.

Mother and calf came together in an embrace of rubbing and caressing, the calf corkscrewing all over his mother's body. Then they wheeled as one, with the calf tucked beneath his mother, snug in her drag-pouch, his tail beating three or four times to each sweep of his mother's as they sped off to join the departing herd.

Gleaming white, then gold, then blue, mother and calf leapt together, each arcing leap taking them further from the turtle's sight until they vanished in a final vault into the sky.

The turtle watched them go, then remembered the comb jelly, and turned just in time to see its flaccid mass sucked into the pouting mouth of a huge Sunfish which rolled one eye towards her before slowly sculling away.

Silence.

In the deep silence born of a tumultuous event, and amplified by the vast emptiness surrounding her, the turtle scanned for food. In the distance a chain of pale yellow lights undulated with the waves and she dived and swam towards them.

She resurfaced a metre or so away from the ribbon of lights, which looked like squid or jellyfish, though not of a kind she had come across before. She hesitated, but her body craved sustenance and she sank level with one light, and opened her mouth to take a bite.

And she saw the bloated bulk of a leatherback turtle a few metres away, entangled in fishing line, with a light-stick lodged firmly in its mouth.

The turtle quickly stroked away, her heart beating fast and loud and her hunger suddenly forgotten.

The Turtles' Tomb

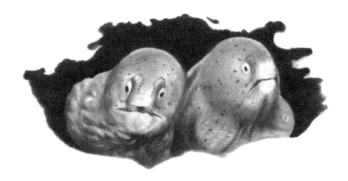

The turtle had scoured the reefs of Sipadan for eighteen days now, with no sight or scent of a male leatherback. But today the urge to mate had become so overwhelming she was determined to suppress her fear and search the dark caves below the black coral line.

She dropped over the edge of a wall draped with orange sponges and plunged through the syrupy slick of the thermocline, pushing against the current sweeping up the cliff face. A carpet of winged mussels stretched the breadth of the rock wall and a black coral tree stood three metres proud of the jagged carpet, with a crown of frost-feathered branches. A ghost pufferfish lounged on the tree's gnarled trunk, its jaundice coloured eyes tracking the turtle's approach, and behind it a dark oval patch on the cliff face marked the entrance to the caves.

The turtle hung in the water, torn between a dread of lurking sharks and her desire to find a mate. A thumping slam suddenly reverberated through the water and she span towards the source of the sound – a giant black parrotfish ramming a tower coral. Almost as long as she was, the fish crunched the coral and swam away, streaming a fine white rain across whorls of whip coral springing in the current.

The turtle pivoted and swam towards the coral tree, gliding over the disinterested pufferfish and into a large, fan-fringed cavern.

Cavebass announced her entrance. Their drumming roll seemed to awaken a black-blotched boulder as a massive potato cod advanced to challenge her, then yawned, belched, and leisurely turned away. The cod's belch bubble spread across the roof of the cave, trembling dead man's fingers, and attracting the attention of lilliputian blind fish who probed for tiny organisms trapped in his air bubbles.

The turtle moved to the centre of the cavern, her eyes adjusting to the absence of light. Relics of a bygone age hung from the ceiling or lay cluttering the floor – Antediluvian stalactites snapped off by quarrelling groupers and nurse sharks. Squirrelfish grunts contoured the cavern's walls and a steady tapping static fell from the ceiling – the territorial dance of hundreds of boxer shrimps, their long signalling antennae poking out past stalactite tips.

The turtle pushed forward, and passed over a mat of glowing fire urchins crowded together in the rear of the cavern. The rear wall blinked bright blue-green at her approach – a vast school of flashlight fish channeling communial courage to send a warning to this gross intruder. She moved towards them and the veil of flashing lights drew apart, revealing a wall plastered with lava flowstone, and in its centre a dark entrance to a labyrinth of tunnels beyond. The leatherback hesitated for just a moment, and then entered the passageway.

After a dozen twists and turns the narrow tunnel ended in a cave so deep in the seamount that no currents stirred its sediment and no light pierced the darkness. The turtle revolved, feeling increasingly uneasy in such a confined space. She sank towards the cave's floor and her flipper tip touched a green turtle's skull, and then her plastron brushed across a pile of bones and empty turtle shells.

Panic welled up in the leatherback and she shoved hard against a floor more bone than rock, bowling turtle skulls as a silt cloud billowed around her. She swept hard, instinctively heading upwards, and crashed into a green turtle cadaver chandeliered on the cave's ceiling.

Now overwhelmed with fear she swept her front flippers and careened into the cave wall, badly grazing her back and flippers. But she ignored the pain, and kept kicking and sweeping, until she suddenly stumbled back into the passageway. Muscles scorched with adrenaline she scrambled along the tunnel, until at last she barged through the shoal of flashlight fish, and swept across the cavern to the open sea. The potato cod hovered in the entrance, and she caught his gills with her flipper tip as she barged past him and bolted for the surface. With her lungs burning for air she pulled and kicked with all her remaining strength and headed up towards white light spears and the aerated clouds of tumbling waves.

She broke surface. And gulped air. Waves smashed

against the island's coastline, no more than a few metres away, and a strong current dragged her past the rocky headland and towards the open sea.

After a while her eyes adjusted to the sun's harsh glare and she noticed a stream of birds bouncing by above, boasting feet of a more brilliant blue than the cloudless sky above them. The boobies were heading for their island homes, laden with crops full of flying fish and squid to chunder into demanding chicks. The turtle followed their flight until they dissolved into shimmering haze and then she turned and dived, and swam hard in the opposite direction, keen to get as far away as she could from the loneliness of the shallow reefs and the sadness of the turtles' tomb of Sipadan.

Aldabra

With her eyes fixed on the cabbage-head jellyfish, the turtle angled her ascent and rose through water warmed by a high summer sun. She gently oared her flippers, taking care not to brush against the tentacles trailing below the pulsing bell and bit, her scissorlike jaws slicing through the glutinous dome. After half a dozen mouthfuls she let the ragged remains sink away, golden glints marking the descent of eight medusa fish dropping with it.

Six years had passed since she swam away from Sipadan and she had spent every breeding season since then searching the oceans for a mate but always in vain, and after each fruitless quest she returned to the only place she knew as home – this emerald atoll of Aldabra, where she would rest and replenish her thick layer of butter fat in preparation for her next trip.

Today the urge to breed was particularly strong and the leatherback was feeding quickly and efficiently, carving many kilos of flesh from her prey.

She dived close to the sandy bottom to seize another jellyfish and a purple triggerfish hurtled towards her stomach, clucking a warning, then he swerved and shot downwards and stood on his head, blowing oxygen over his egg clutch.

A jellyfish brushed across the turtle's beaklike mouth and she tore chunks from its bell, and snipped and swallowed its tentacles.

And as she rose to take another bite she caught a glimpse of a plump pink throat pouch, and a black paddle, slightly smaller than her own.

And then the jellyfish sank beneath her line of sight and she could clearly see the concave plastron and thick extended tail of a male leatherback turtle.

After three or four fumbled attempts the male leatherback succeeded in mounting the female and joined together they rode the tidal river racing through Aldabra's Grande Passe, buffeted by white-horsed water surging at six knots or more.

Two metres below them streaks of ivory rock glared through the dunes of the sea bed, and dark patches of dead coral, pummelled by the current which tore through the pass twice a day.

With a sudden acceleration they swept into a canyon, some fifteen metres across, with steep vertical walls. The floor bulged up to within a few metres of the surface then sharply fell away to thirty metres, several times. The tidal race was at its strongest here and the turtles pitched and lurched through murky water, both forced to tilt and trim constantly to remain balanced, and joined.

They entered the Inner Lagoon and the female forced the male turtle to the surface, drew breath and dropped again, barging through a school of red and yellow grunts.

She snatched her next breath in water whirling and churning against the undercut base of Round Table

Islet as the current carried them beneath the black rock cap and the male pushed hard against the mushroom-stem, sending a wavelet lapping across a partially submerged ledge and glossing a trio of red and blue crabs grappling over a disinterested female. The scimitar winged shadow of a frigatebird flittered across the crabs and they scrambled back beneath the surface, the need for refuge suddenly taking precedence over reproduction.

Hot and heavy air smothered the casuarina trees crowding the islet, which spluttered with the cries of red and white-tailed tropicbirds squabbling over nesting space, and in the oppressive heat of high summer creatures bold in colour and intention toiled to breed and reproduce. A few hundred metres away from the coupled turtles, where water gargled and popped against a mudcurb, a sacred ibis speared a flounder, and lifted its flapping prize high in the air, then dunked it back in the water, dabbling it free of mud before turning and presenting it to his intended mate. Beyond the ibis the slate grey mud flats stuttered with the sexual semaphore of mudskippers flicking their brightly coloured dorsal fins to attract a mate, while jostling for space with male fiddler crabs beckoning females with a scarlet come-hither wave.

The turtles drifted past the mud flats and their shadows rippled across an extended family of garden eels, many hundreds strong, who slid gracefully into their mud hole homes, and only ventured out again when the turtles had gone, to reweave their vast carpet of swaying crooks, all curling in one direction, questioning the current.

The mangrove forest stretched ahead and the lagoon floor dropped away into a wide trough, gouged by current and tide, and hedged by the prop and buttress roots of red mangroves. The turtles drifted on, their progress tracked by a squad of golden-eyed stingrays buried wingtip-to-wingtip in the sandy mud below; a communal ambush for berried lobsters.

The turtles cleared the trough and entered the world of the sea trees, a world of gurgles and murmurs, and cool jade water, stitched with stilt roots and dapple shaded by arched, lead-grey branch umbrellas.

The male's ridged back snagged in a root parasol, and the female's rear paddles dragged through the mud, dredging up a black cloud of silt and leaf litter. Colourless globules of gas rose to the surface and burst with a rotten, pungent smell, and an archerfish rose beside them, and spat a volley of droplets at a newly emerged emperor dragonfly, wings still wet and crumpled, clinging to an overhanging branch two feet above. The waterdrops punched the black and gold insect into the air and it tumbled down the male turtle's back and into the water, where it was instantly devoured.

An hour later the turtles were deep within the mangrove maze, in water so still and clear it had no surface, and no depth.

Dusk seeped through the mangrove canopy while a rabble of fruit bats chattered and preened in preparation for that night's long flight. Neon-sparkler clouds of fireflies danced in a clearing beneath the apple trees and a convoy of egg-laden robber crabs lumbered along the edge of the mud bank, heading for the Inner Lagoon. Baby oysters closed their hairy shells. And the leatherback turtles slept soundly, joined together in a jasmine scented world of soft mud and cool water.

The female turtle awoke. The male had gone. Grey dampness drizzled through the canopy and the sky was filled with the whomping sounds of slashing leather wings as bats streamed back to roost, their bellies full from feasting on the fruits of a more bountiful island, three hours flight away.

One overfull bat crash-landed into a tree above the turtle, dislodging ripe fruit, and proclaiming his return

with raucous, high-pitched cries. Then he clapped his wings and inverted himself, and sidestepped along the bough, and stopped where the branch forked and a thick tangle of leaves provided a little protection from sun and rain.

The turtle raised her head. A sweet smell wafted out from the mud bank and the insistent din of wasps and horseflies grew louder as the bell-dome silhouette of a giant tortoise plodded towards her.

The giant tortoise's shell seemed to deflate in a punctured hiss as he splayed his legs and extended his three foot neck to reach a mangrove apple speared on a cone root. The splintered claws of his forelegs sank into the mud curb and chiselled away a leaf mould wedge which slid beneath the surface, exposing three popcorn shrimps which were immediately sucked whole into the mouth of a passing red snapper.

Sucking, gum-slapping sounds drowned out the whining insects as the tortoise's fat tongue rolled the ripe apple to the back of his throat. Dribble oozed from his flat chin, and the sticky tip of his tongue, stained scarlet by Hibiscus flowers, slopped over stumps of brown teeth and curled upwards to collect a gob of mashed apple clogging one nostril. Then he stretched out his turkey neck of saggy, deep creased skin, and nudged his mallet nose into the lens of fresh water overlaying the sea, and drank through his nostrils.

A fig stone passed by the fruit bat plopped into the water in front of the turtle and the tortoise swung his neck towards the disturbance, his scuffed face so close to the turtle's that she could taste the apple on his breath, and see the milky opaqueness of cataracts fogging his thick-lidded eyes.

A thick mat of algae teeming with spiny lobster larvae bumped into the tortoise's face, and he sniffed it, and took a bite, and leisurely chomped away. The algae mat twirled out of the tortoise's reach and he lifted his head and raised his body high in a casual tortoise stretch, rocking from side to side. Then he yawned and slowly swung away, creaking and swaying, impatient to stake a claim in his favourite mud hollow and coat his body in tick-entrapping mud before finding a shady spot for his midday siesta.

And that evening he would join many thousands of his kind gathered in the grasslands of the West, where he would roar and bellow, and clash and clank, and seize every chance he could to mount and mate, just as he had done every breeding season for the last one

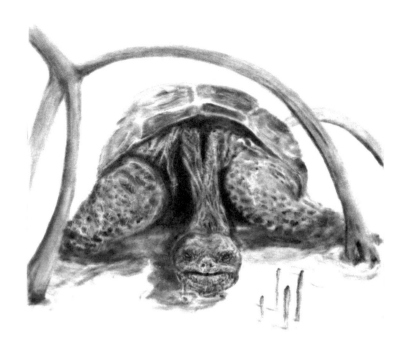

hundred and thirty eight years.

The turtle turned and swam with the flow of greasy water draining from the mangrove swamp, back through the maze of roots to Johnny's Channel.

She broke surface in the Inner Lagoon and swam slowly along the edge of the mud flats, past a battalion of soldier crabs retreating before a stand of crab plovers, their heavy dagger bills cocked in front, while a little further along a fishing skink gorged on bunches of robber crab eggs deposited the previous evening.

Bloated black clouds rumbled and belched, spewing rain, and swelling the billions of gallons of seawater draining from the Inner lagoon where waterfalls now poured from islets and tiers of coral, and merged with cascading rapids and rivulets flowing into larger fish-bone streams and on to the Grande Passe spine.

The turtle stayed on the surface, and surfed the choppy waters funnelling out through the main channel, where a quivering net of fish stretched the full width of the channel, each knot a glassnose or razorbelly, harvesting the rich bouillabaisse of eggs and larvae flushed out by the tide, while a pack of trevally hunted the sandstorm below as the fast flowing efflux stripped the cover from small crustaceans and invertebrates.

The strong current carried the turtle to the edge of the drop-off, where sapphire water bruised to deep blue, and the white cave-mouths of manta rays trawled the planktonic broth, their immense looping wings kissing the surface as they curled into a graceful slow motion backward somersault and dropped to rejoin the feeding wheel below.

The turtle was keen to begin her long journey but the air pressure and wave roll told her she would be heading into the full force of an approaching storm and she was unwilling to take any risks with the sparks of new life in her belly.

She breathed deeply and dived, heading for the deep water below the black coral line, where she would have to find a safe place to wait for the storm to pass.

The turtle hovered and stared at the shipwreck's silhouette, etched with straight lines and angles forged in another world. A tropical cyclone had broken the trawler's back many years ago, and she now lay on a bed of crumpled iron sheets, her wooden decks and masts long since rotted away. But her enormous bronze propeller stood proud of the twisted metal, its edges blurred by batfish weaving between the blades.

The turtle swam along the ship's bow, which was still fairly intact, and into a galleyway packed with a dense shoal of anchovies. The shoal swayed and contoured around her until she entered the wheel-house and brushed against the coral encrusted telegraph, sending a tremor through the wheelhouse floor. An old painted lobster recoiled in alarm at such a rare disturbance and a dragon moray unwound from the wheel, bared his fangs, and threaded through a tear in the wall.

The turtle dropped to the floor. The touch of steel was cold on her skin and a surge of silt puffed across an octopus nestled beneath a bulkhead. Glowing with a mother of pearl radiance the octopus assessed the turtle intruder then resumed her maternal duties, studiously cleaning each of the many dozens of pouches dangling from the shelf behind her, delicate pressure from her suckers plucking dirt from each egg sacs' surface and sending a message of reassurance to her offspring wriggling within. Her three hearts worked hard as she swelled and puffed, and gently blew water from her siphons across the shivering membranes; a dying mother's gift of aeration to her babies struggling to break free.

The turtle tucked her flippers and lowered her head. A ripple of sinuous motion marked the dragon moray's return, and the painted lobster's antennae twitched in the turtle's direction. But the normal sounds of the sea were hushed here, in this world within itself, and the turtle closed her eyes.

And in silence she waited for the storm.

The Storm

All that night the tempest raged, hurling huge waves against Aldabra's reefs, pounding and pummelling ancient coral. Typhonic winds whipped across the Inner Lagoon, churning shallow water to foam, flinging sand and stones across the mud flats, clogging mudskipper burrows and drowning the occupants entombed below.

Screaming gusts of ninety miles an hour shredded the mangrove canopy, snapping branches and stripping leaves, and tossing them into the swirling water, where they buried rootlets and seedlings, and oysters and fish fry.

Fruit bats huddled in scrums of many hundreds and the giant tortoises hunkered down wherever they were when the storm hit, lest they lose their way in the blinding rain and stumble into potholes in the champignon rock, or wander into the lagoon and be swept out to sea.

Feathertail stingrays and blacktip shark pups exited the lagoon to cluster around the shipwreck. And the turtle left her sanctuary only once during the storm, to breach through tumbling waves and flush her lungs with spume-whipped air.

Shortly after dawn she rose through murky water spiced with the tang of the terrestrial world and broke surface as the rain ceased and sunlight slashed the grey sky, reflecting off the fish-oiled plumage of a spiral of many thousands of fairy terns, bestowing the lagoon with a halo of brilliant white.

Spent clouds scudded away. A warm breeze blew out from Aldabra, wrinkling the surface, and three flamingoes thumped by above, legs trailing.

A coconut with a silk spider stowaway bobbed past the turtle's head, and she turned and swept her flippers in a graceful arc, heading in the same direction as the wind-blown clouds, away from Aldabra, westwards, towards the beach of her birth.

Tiger Shark

The turtle awoke.

What had disturbed her sleep she did not know, perhaps a quake on a far off seabed, or the throb of a ship's propellers, or some intuitive sense of the danger rising from below.

She dipped her head and peered into a

plankton fog flickering with the light pores of feeding lanternfish. Below the plankton bloom a faint coloured glow was emanating from the depths, rapidly growing in radiance and intensity. The turtle raised her head to breathe, and the moonlit swell seemed to shatter into silver-green splinters as thousands of lanternfish erupted from the waves and rained back down.

The turtle swept her flippers and dived, now fully alert, for she had been in a position like this before and she knew what was coming. She lunged and barged through the dense confusion of fish and broke into water sparkling with emerald diatoms and the opalescent barrels of comb jellies.

Then salvoes of red and yellow rockets flared up from the depths as squid up to a metre long punched holes in the lanternfish shoal, clubbing and hooking, snaring and seizing, and then dropping away, their tentacles bucking with the ineffectual escape attempts of the prey wrapped within. Others hung vertically and dexterously filleted their food, discarding heads and guts, the water blood-clouded by their labours. The severed head of one large lanternfish dropped past the turtle's face, its luminous light pores still glowing, until it faded into black.

But the black wore ribbons of blue-green phosphorescence. As the turtle had discovered before, whenever squid massed in such numbers, the sharks would come.

The blue shark twitched. A shudder ran the length of its slender body and it surged upwards, tail sweeping hard and fast as it drove straight into the mass of squid and fish. Detonations of ink puffed all around the turtle as the squid took evasive actions – quicksilver fast, tight movements, swift changes of direction, sharp, sudden bursts of acceleration and abrupt stops.

Scores of sharks shot past the turtle and piled into the squid, slashing and snapping, popping some bodies and wolfing others whole. True gluttons of the sea, many gorged past their stomach's capacity and regurgitated what they had already taken, and started feasting again.

Then whorls of phosphorescence spun past her as a deep water thresher shark joined the fray. The shark swam side-on to its targets, whipping its four foot high scimitar tail, flailing and swatting, then cruising back along its path to collect its stunned and crippled prey.

The turtle banked hard and swam away, determined to put a safe distance between herself and the expanding frenzy. The blue sharks would not target her deliberately, but in their voracious haste they could snap at her flippers, or take a swipe at her head.

She stretched her flippers in preparation for a full powerstroke, and froze. A tiger shark was stalking her, eyes glinting, and glowing green outline tracing ever-tightening circles. The turtle fought the urge to bolt, knowing she could not outswim the shark and that any panicked movements would entice and arouse it. The shark closed to within twelve metres of her and she could see the true size of the ocean prowler – at least four times her own length. The turtle held her nerve, carefully tilted both rear paddles, relaxed her fore flippers, and began to drop.

The tiger shark followed her, leisurely descending in a spiral of decreasing circles, seemingly content to wait and see what she would do before making his move.

At five hundred metres below sea level the shark dropped beneath her – its favoured angle of attack. With her head drooped the turtle watched the predator's approach, its sleek and powerful bulk sheathed in cold blue radiance, and balanced waves of sinuous movement culminating in precise sideways sweeps of its tail.

At six hundred metres the shark moved in. Its first exploratory pass was so close that the turtle felt the pressure change of its motion, and on the return pass she saw its gill slits flare, and felt the rasping kiss of a pectoral fin.

At seven hundred metres the shark swept up and past once more, and tail-slapped the turtle's side, twirling her round, daring her to flee, but the turtle knew that any sudden movements would invite a ferocious and fatal attack so she simply span and sank even faster.

At eight hundred metres she dropped past packs of cock-eyed squid – sculling thunderclouds which challenged one another with flashes of yellow photophores or pumped dark ink into hollow mantle cavities to extinguish all lights. A cockatoo squid brushed her side and immediately bolted away, blazing green flames and ejecting a glowing cloud of luminous ink which shivered and densified, mimicking the shape of the now distant impressionist.

At nine hundred metres the shark headed directly for her, and bumped her hard with its snout in the soft flesh of her throat pouch. She lurched backwards, then toppled over and dropped into darkness, her flippers bent upwards in the rapid momentum of her descent.

The turtle plunged through one thousand metres, the deepest she had ever been. She had not taken in sufficient air for a descent to this depth and now the rapidly increasing water pressure began to compress her lungs.

The shark circled just above her and headed towards her again, but this time its approach was lazier and less determined, as if the darkness and the turtle's lack of response had dulled its interest.

At eleven hundred metres the turtle tumbled through the midst of a black swarm pulsing with bright blue and red spheres – the eyes and wing tips of a vast flock of vampire squid, flapping their spread cape fins, reluctantly breaking formation to allow her through. Her flipper tip poked a globular eyeball and the squid instantly ejected a brilliant blue mucus, filled with tiny glowing balls, a glitter storm which swirled all over her and quickly faded away.

At twelve hundred metres the frigid water had a waxen opaqueness which confused the turtle's senses and frustrated her eyes. The few lights visible came from creatures which hunted and hid and bred and died here – flashes and bursts of red, blue and green, streaking and vanishing. Bioluminescence to identify and beckon, illuminate and threaten. Puffs and clouds of precious light to communicate and challenge, deceive and escape.

At fifteen hundred metres the coldest water the turtle had ever known burned her entire body. Her thick layer of insulating fat calloused and cracked, and fatigue-injecting cold gnawed through flesh and blood, chilling the new life developing in her reproductive tract. A vague spherical outline pulsed close by; eleven metres across, a deep crimson bell rimmed in shocking pink and trailing twenty metre long diaphanous tentacles. The turtle dropped only inches away from it, her cold-slugged brain incapable of executing an evasive manoeuvre, unaware that the briefest touch of one shimmering venom sac would instantly fuse every nerve in her body.

At sixteen hundred metres she briefly felt the sonar clicks of a sperm whale hunting below, their echoes sketching a sound map to guide him through abyssal canyons draped with the frozen flows of ancient lava.

At eighteen hundred metres bitter cold stung and

cramped her muscles, sucking the last trace of warmth from her blood. The crushing weight of water clamped the turtle's carapace tight against her plastron and her semi-rigid chest collapsed. A pressure spike bored into her skull where the fox's tooth had penetrated, and she began to slide into unconsciousness.

At two kilometres below sea level, a mere one hundred metres above the seabed, she sank towards a cold floor carpetted with the summer's plankton bloom and grazed by herds of giant spider crabs. The sperm whale cruised by, his mouth held open as he tongue-squeezed squid between his teeth, aggravating his brilliant lure – a glowing cephalopod paste which coated his teeth and glossed his lips, coaxing curious prey within range.

The turtle's flippers hung limp, unable to function on their meagre ration of cold blood, and twitching uncontrollably as compressed nerves fired messages to redundant muscles. Her core body temperature was now so low she was on the edge of toppling into a state of cold stunning, and in a matter of moments she would be chill-crippled past the point of recovery. Another degree colder and her body would enter irreversible shut down.

She dropped another few metres, past a ragged pillar of crumbling rock, its peak plumed with fern corals, and its sides stubbled with tubeworms. Hordes of blind squat lobsters weaved between the worms wrinkled organ pipe homes, tapping for limpets. The turtle brushed against the tip of a stinging, fleshy sea pen, and felt nothing.

Suddenly a loud clang vibrated through the water. Then another boom of sound, and another, closer still, shook her body. The sperm whale was nearing the end of his dive and hunting at maximum pace, casting his deepest tones to flick on lights in the bodies of unseen squid. Another concentrated burst of bass creaks sent needles of sound through her flesh and bone, penetrating her stupor, and in a sluggish, semi-conscious motion, she tilted and lurched upwards.

Twelve minutes later she burst through the surface, heave breathing. She fanned her flippers and paddled to stay afloat, shivering and regurgitating partially digested jellyfish which snagged against the barbs in her throat and gagged her, and made her retch again.

Warmth and sensation began to return to her body, but with the return of feeling came the burning pain of the sea pen's sting, and a fierce, cold-induced hunger. She dipped her head and scanned for food. Silver glints to her left marked the presence of a resting oarfish, gently rotating her long ventral rays, and a few shivers of phosphorescene etched a sea snake's trail. But she could see no pulsing lights of jellyfish, just a pale white glow, rising from the darkness. The turtle stared, transfixed, as the light grew steadily stronger, and then the blunt head of a Sperm whale filled her vision, his glowing white lips dribbling luminescence.

For the next few hours the turtle stayed by the whale's side, trembling in the rumbling sounds of squid digestion until the first light of dawn brought dimension and detail to the leviathan's bulk. From cliff head to scalloped tail he was just under twenty metres long, three metres of which were taken up by a flat mouth crammed with a muscle-tongue and two dozen pairs of peg teeth.

A livid chinstrap of giant squid sucker rings radiated out from each side of his underslung jaw, beneath which four sharksuckers clung, waving lazily, their disc

shaped heads fastened tight against his skin.

Scars and scratches covered the behemoth's oak bark skin, and massive muscles bulged at his tapered end – the power unit to drive the tail, to propel forty tonnes of bulk.

The sun had not yet cleared the horizon when a crack of sound shook the turtle, and a vented spume of oily, foul smelling breath showered across her. Next came the roar of the recoiling inhalation, S-blowhole stretched wide and air screaming down the windpipe, soaking quivering lungs and saturating muscles with oxygen.

After another twenty-nine repetitions the whale's immense tail flukes rose in a deliberate arc, and rainbow sheets of phosphorescent flecked water cascaded down as his tail touched vertical, and pistoned down. His first tail sweep thrust a ring of expanding smooth water up and outwards, rimmed with turbulence, his own unique flukeprint, while bubble chains twirled up towards the turtle and her pilot fish darted between them, snapping at flakes of shed whale skin.

The turtle watched the whale melt into midnight blue and then she stretched and swept her front flippers, awkwardly at first, but after a few strokes she settled into a fluid, consistent rhythm; an energy efficient motion to carry her and her developing embryos across more than three thousand kilometres of open ocean, with little time to rest or feed, and swimming against the current.

Part Three

The Eagle Owl

The eagle owl reached the cliff face, fanned her wings, and rose swiftly on a spiralling updraft as chilled desert air swept against the heat retaining rock.

At six hundred feet above sea level she tucked her wings, thrust out her moon-booted legs and alighted silently on a dew pocked ledge. She bowed her head to peck at a louse gnawing her chest then shook and settled her feathers, and waddled into the eyrie.

Two puffballs of grey down were huddled together in the centre of the nest chamber, and bone and feather pellets littered the floor. The eagle owl scooped up one pellet, backed out of the chamber, and flicked the remains of the reed warbler over the ledge to land amongst the rocks below.

A scraping sound came from behind her and she swivelled her head and stared into the glowing orange irises of her largest chick, who was now hissing and clacking her beak, demanding to be fed. But the eagle owl's talons were empty, and since the recent death of her lifelong mate she had managed to deliver only one warbler, two gerbils, and a few beetles and spiders to her starving offspring.

The other owlet slept on. Four days smaller than his sibling, he was now critically malnourished and tomorrow or the day after he would die and be devoured by his sibling if his mother could not provide more sustenance.

The eagle owl turned and dropped from the ledge.

A single wing beat took her away from the cliff face and out over the dunes.

With the new day approaching she had barely enough time for one last sweep of the beach before buzzards and steppe eagles would begin to converge on the cliffs, soaring on the thermals to search for unguarded rock dove nests and clumsy virgin flight fledglings.

The eagle owl flew in total silence, velvet feathers on the cutting edges of her wings muffling the air rushing over them as her horned ears filtered out bat trills and cicada-chirr, her hearing tuned to detect the rustling of a courser or a sandgrouse, while her eyes scanned the sand in ultra-violet for gerbil urine tracks.

With no signs or sounds of prey apparent she banked right and pumped her wings, and headed towards the dull expanse of the sand drifts.

Half way through her second sweep of the drifts a slight movement on a distant crest caught her attention and she wheeled in a tight winged loop, and chopped the air a little harder than before.

Two hundred metres

from the crest she swerved to avoid a mouse-tailed bat then tilted her wings and began a swift and silent descent.

The agama lizard paused on the drift crest and cleared sand grains from his eyes with a careful rolling of his long tongue. Stiff and sluggish from the chilly night breeze he would have to hurry if he was to reach the safety of his favourite sun basking ledge before dawn. He lifted his belly clear of the sand and swaggered down the drift face, spiny scaled toes kicking up tiny spurts of sand and forked tongue flicking out and in.

Suddenly his mouth sprang open, his legs buckled, and his eyes bulged as razor sharp talons tore through his flesh. But the pain lasted for only an instant before his spine snapped under the massive shock of the impact.

The sheer speed of the eagle owl's attack had driven one talon through the roof of the lizard's skull and she tumbled forward, three sickle claws caught in its scaly skin. She knew that a fully grown agama could inflict serious injury on an eagle owl and she had hit the lizard at full speed to ensure an outright kill.

Shaking the sand from her feathers she ripped her talons free, hopped backwards, and glowered down at her prey writhing on the sand, its tail thrashing from side to side. A beetle's crushed carapace, black with white spots, spewed from its mouth. Then the lizard bucked and twitched, and lay still.

The eagle owl stepped on to the lizard, expertly selecting a balanced grip for her flight, and stretched her wings. Clouds of sand billowed around her as she rose clear and swung away towards the cliffs, wings pumping hard and talons spread wide to carry her heavy prize back to her offspring.

The Boy

The boy trembled with excitement as he watched the eagle owl disappear into the dark mass of the cliffs, then he slapped at a mosquito gorging on the back of his hand and walked across to see what was fluttering in a desert rose shrub a few feet away from where the lizard had died. He reached the bush and bent down, and carefully pulled an exquisite tawny feather speckled with gold from the thorns of the brier bush. He stroked a few crooked barbs back into line and smiled, delighted with his find, and happy for the owl's success.

The fluting whistles of a hoopoe lark spiralled up from the far side of the dunes and the boy stood still and listened, trying to pinpoint the dawn piper's exact location. But he was too tired and hungry to really concentrate and he knew he could delay no longer if he was to reach the fishing village and be back before sunset. He turned and walked back down the tidal plain to his fishing boat and grabbed a bottle of water and his empty petrol can. The engine had spluttered and died three hours before and his shoulders and back still ached from the effort of rowing his tin boat to shore. There was only one village along this twenty mile stretch of coastline and he was lucky that the currents had carried him in the right direction. His father and uncles were known in the village and the fishermen would give him fuel for his boat, and cheese and bread to eat, and maybe even some of their delicious dates to take home for his mother. She would be too busy dealing with his seven siblings to notice his absence until that evening and if Allah was merciful he would be home by then, with his pockets full of dates and his baskets crammed with crayfish from the pots he had set on the offshore reefs.

A skein of cranes piped overhead, heading North, and the boy turned and jogged towards the village, determined to cover as many miles as he could before the heat of midday made travel impossible. He smiled as he thought about how happy his mother would be when he gave her the dates, and his smile grew wider still as he thought about the fun he would have getting his own back on the brother who had swopped his full fuel can for an empty one.

The Drift Net

For two days and nights a virus had blocked the turtle's sinuses, slowing her progress and preventing her from diving to search for food, or to escape the baking sun. And now she was forced to endure a guano hailstorm as millions upon millions of birds passed overhead; Bee-eaters, rollers, swallows, swifts and wagtails, streaming along an avian flyway in birds-of-a-feather layers so thick that they made this August midday as dark and clamorous as Aldabra's mangrove forest at twilight.

An exhausted Indian Roller fell from one chain, twirling and somersaulting, and vanished into a wave trough, a scrawny mouthful for the next roving shark or great barracuda. But a moment later the bird's brilliant blue body appeared atop the next wave crest, impaled on a spike sticking up from a drift net.

The turtle approached the net and stopped. Unable to dive below its thirty metre depth she turned with the current and swam slowly along its length.

A few minutes later she came across the net's first victim – a mature and mostly intact silvertip shark, snared by the gills. A little further along hung a hammerhead, and then a huge sunfish, smothered in a nylon cocoon. Next - A black marlin, six hundred kilos strong, sailfin twisted and torn. Then two hawksbill turtles.

The turtle swam on, past the grey and pasty stumps of shark heads, their bodies chopped away by canni-balistic brethren, and more mutilated billfish and barracuda. But no tuna, the net's target catch.

Later that morning she came across the first dolphin carcass, hanging snout down, fins tied tight against its body. Dead less than an hour no sharks had yet claimed it. This young female marked the outer edge of a circle within which five more adult dolphins hung. And one calf.

The calf had died just a few minutes before and his mottled body still twitched and jerked, his mouth lashed laughing-open. His mother hung next to him, emitting a pitiful mewing sound which entered the same empty spaces in the turtle's body that the calf's calls had a few weeks before, but this time the cries

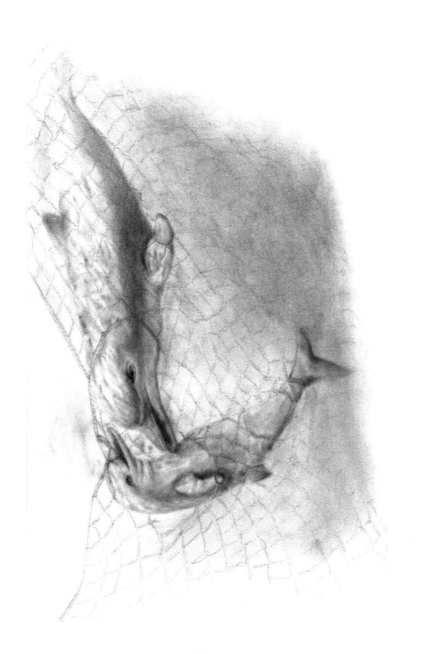

were so high pitched and intense they felt like fire urchin spines searing her stomach and sinuses.

The mother gently nudged her offspring's dead body, and sighed a rasping burr, pleading with him to break free. Then she caressed his face with her limp lower jaw, fractured in three places. Puffs of blood twirled up from her mouth, lacerated by broken teeth where she had worried the unyielding mesh. Then her head slumped, her pleading ceased, and she died, wrapped in a nylon shroud, unable to break the cords that bound her calf, or the bond that held her to him.

The turtle reached the net's edge and paused to rest and check her bearings. Her forced powerswim across three thousand kilometres of ocean and the debilitating effects of the virus had left her craving food and sleep, and her body had begun to feed on itself, absorbing her layer of butter-fat insulation. But rest and nourishment would have to wait. First she had a beach to find, and a nest to dig, and eggs to lay.

Behind her the death-web drifted on, to mindlessly snare more victims until their total weight became too great for the floats to bear and dragged the net down to rest, but not rot, on the sea bed.

The Boy and the Turtle

Sunset.

Twilight signalled the end of the sight hunters day and the sea now belonged to the touchers and the scent stalkers, probing sand and coral and tasting the water for the faint chemical traces of prey. Bigeyes, crabs and crayfish, soldierfish and squirrelfish, starfish and urchins, searched and scoured the reef, sweeping up the day's dead, the dying and the infirm.

All over the reef shoals of glittering jewelfish surrendered their feeding zones to nestle deep within palmate coral speckled with the silver glows of grinning Tiger cardinalfish, their mouths stuffed with brooding eggs. And directly below the turtle a sinuous convoy of queen parrotfish threaded through a bed of giant clams, beak to tailfin, heading for the dark shelter of deep water.

The turtle felt the burring clicks of bottlenose dolphins resting nearby, half of each cetaceans' brain

105

held in suspension while the other half ticked over, alert to danger. She felt the thud of a clown triggerfish ramming himself into a crevice in the reef face and unsheathing and erecting his dorsal spine, locking himself in his rock refuge. She felt the thrum of a marbled ray waddling by, then dropping to electro-cute a slipper lobster scavenging in a sand patch below. And she felt the weight of new life in her womb.

She broke surface beneath cliffs etched with the oyster burnish of a full moon and gazed towards a land she had last seen seventeen years before.

A bird's flint cry bounced off the cliff face and the turtle paused, alert for any sign of danger, then she swam slowly towards the beach until her flippers hoed the sloping sand and seawater spilled from her back.

Her eyes struggled to adjust to this terrestrial world as she hauled herself out of the sea and stumbled, her flippers bowing under the great weight of her body, suddenly subjected to gravity's punishing load.

The turtle wrenched her flippers free of the sand's suction and shoved hard with her back paddles, heaving her barrel body across the clinging wet sand half a dozen times before slumping down on the seaweed and shells of the strandline. A wheezing snort bubbled from her flared nostrils, alarming hordes of ghost crabs sifting sand all around her, and the alien aroma of a decaying hammerhead shark stung the insides of nostrils too delicate for such an odour.

She hoisted her front end and heaved her five hundred kilo bulk across the rippled bars of a plain she had so nearly died on as a hatchling, away from her ocean home and towards the dark silhouettes of dunes in the distance.

The boy trudged up the dune's flank, breathing heavily, and stood on the crest. He wiped the sweat from his forehead, and placed the petrol can on the sand while he cursed himself yet again for having slept the afternoon away in the cool shade of an Umbrella tree. The pealing voice of the local Iman calling the faithful to evening prayers had woken him and when he finally reached the village the villagers were celebrating a wedding and had insisted he stayed to gorge himself on coconut fish curry and fried bananas.

He licked his lips at the memory of the feast then took a swig of water and stomped down the dune's slope with sand rivulets hissing all around him.

Just then, a growling noise came from the darkness and the boy slid to a halt at the base of the dune, shin deep in an avalanche of soft sand. Another moan fouled the silence and the boy felt the hairs rise on his arms and the heat drain from his cheeks.

He shivered, imagining fierce crocodiles, and peered into the gloom, and could just make out the moonlit outline of a large hump at the base of the next dune. But the hump was oval, and there was no sign of huge jaws, or a long tail. The boy pulled his feet free, took two deep breaths, and walked across to the hump.

At first the boy could not believe his eyes. He had heard so many stories about the creature lying before him, and longed to see one for so long that for a moment he thought he must be dreaming. But then the animal sighed, and flapped a wing flipper, and the boy could smell her breath, and feel the tremors of her movement, and he knew that she was real. And he knew what she was. She was a dinosaur, come to life. She was a giant sea turtle!

The boy stood and stared at the turtle, his eyes wide and soaking in every detail from her jagged beak mouth and blubbery shoulders to the seven sawtoothed keels running the length of her carapace, and the great wing flippers half buried by her sides.

The turtle groaned, and a tear bulged from beneath her thick eyelid, shining bright with a tiny stud moon. The boy crouched by the turtle's side and gently brushed sand from a dent on her head. She blinked, and another salt filled tear rolled down her cheek, and the boy thought about how far away from her home she was, and how incredibly hard it must have been for her to haul her heavy body up the beach. And his lips stretched into a broad, joyful smile, and his eyes glistened with admiration for the magnificent creature before him.

The turtle hiccupped, and her udder like throat quivered. Her rear end shifted, and the boy shuffled round to her tail and leaned forward to peer into the hole between her splayed paddles. A clutch of a dozen or so chalk coloured eggs covered the bottom of a smooth sided chamber and the boy carefully reached down and picked one up. The turtle sighed again and settled, and the boy sat cross legged and stared at the warm soft-shelled egg cupped in his hands.

And while the leatherback laid her eggs, the boy breathed in great draughts of turtle scent, and felt a rush of remembered delight for the wonderful stories his grandfather used to tell him, stories about moonbright summer nights when bales of giant turtles would crowd the beach, and the fishermen would fill many baskets with turtle eggs to trade for sweet bananas and coconuts from the farmers, and frankincense and cooking pots from the sailors, eager for the eggs' potency to please pretty ladies and sire sons.

And he remembered the tales his father used to tell, tales about when he was a boy and he and his brothers would come to this bay for a week every

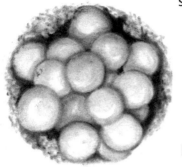

summer to fish and sleep all day, and patrol the beach each night, waiting and watching for the turtle's eggs to hatch. And he remembered how his father could make hand-shadow hatchlings swim through a campfire's glow, and how his eyes would shine and his voice would soar when he spoke about charging all over the beach to rescue baby turtles from swarms of seabirds, and racing along the edge of the sea to snatch hatchlings from the claws of spectral ghost crabs.

But bedtime stories belonged to the past now. And so, said his father, did the turtles.

The giant turtles had last been seen seventeen years ago, five years before the boy was born. No leatherbacks had been spotted in the archipelago since then, none had been caught in the fishing nets, and no nests had been found. The fishermen and villagers all agreed that the giant turtles had all died or gone elsewhere, and abandoned this nesting-site; the last leatherback rookery in the islands.

The boy placed the egg back in the nest and sat silently while the turtle strained and snorted, and laid another seventy two eggs in the nest chamber.

When the last egg had been laid the turtle sighed and shovelled sand with her rear paddles until the chamber was full. Then a loud hiss escaped from her mouth as her plastron expanded and she hoisted herself out of her body pit, and swept and flung more sand to camouflage the nest. Then she lay still for a while, wheezing and gathering her strength, until the call of the sea overcame her weariness and she raised her heavy torso and pitched forward, and the beach shook beneath the boy's bottom as the turtle's body thumped down.

The boy rose and walked by the turtle's side, matching her laborious pace as she heaved and hauled herself towards the sea, only able to manage two or three lunges at a time before exhaustion forced her to halt and recover.

She had covered just over half the distance to the sea when she slumped down and lay still for far longer than before, with her flippers and throat pouch spread across the sand.

The boy knelt beside her, his face only a few inches from her crimson cheek. Her thick lidded eyes stared blankly ahead and her breathing sounded strained and painful, and smelt like dead urchins did before the ants devoured them.

The boy gazed into the turtle's bloodshot eye, and his heart ached for a creature that could neither comprehend nor return his compassion. He would never know what hardships she had overcome or how far she had travelled to lay her eggs in the beach of her birth, but he did know that she was a survivor against the odds, and she was one of the amazing animals he had read so much about but had never expected to see. She was a Tiger, an Elephant, and a Polar bear. She was one of the last of her kind. And she was the Ocean, made flesh.

The boy placed his hand on the turtle's back. Her flesh felt hot, alarmingly so, and the dent on her head glared livid red. The boy knew that if she remained on the beach she would bake in the sun, or fall prey to dogs and buzzards. But he also knew that he was not strong enough to get her to the sea on his own, and there was no one who could help for many miles around.

He raised his head and looked towards the sea, then back at the carmine curves of the sand dunes.

Then he sprang to his feet and ran back into the dunes, to where he had left his fuel can and water bottle. He paused just long enough to take two big swallows of water before running down to the sea and thrusting the bottle beneath the surface.

When the last air bubble had bulged from the bottle's neck the boy ran back to the turtle and dropped to his knees in front of her, and carefully poured the cool seawater across her salt encrusted eyelids.

The turtle's eyelids twitched, and she blinked, slowly and stickily at first, but then more freely as the water washed the guck from her eyes. The boy kept pouring until the bottle was empty, then he ran back to the sea and refilled it.

He poured the second saltwater dose all over the turtle's head, and as it cascaded down her ruddy cheeks she gulped and gurgled, and the boy grinned with relief, and aimed the stream of cool water into her gaping mouth.

When the flow of water from the third bottleful had ceased, the leatherback hiccupped, and held her head proud of the sand, and the boy was sure she had regained her awareness of the sea ahead.

He moved to her rear and bent down and pushed, and the turtle growled, and snorted, but didn't move an inch. The boy linked his fingers and lifted the pointed end of her carapace and shoved again, and the turtle juddered, and pushed with her rear paddles, and moved a third of a body length closer to the sea.

And as the leatherback turtle and the boy staggered across the plain, wisps of pale fog drifted over them, salting the boy's thirst and weaving water beads through his hair. The sea-spiced mist filled the turtle's mouth and nostrils and she began to advance under her own power, and the boy let go, and followed a few feet behind as she thumped down the tidal slope, churning sand and bulldozing ghost crab pyramids, until the sea swept up the slope to greet her, and she slapped through the shallows and out into the bay.

The boy stood at the sea's edge and watched the turtle cut through the water with butterfly strokes of astonishing power and elegance. She raised her head to breathe just before the coral reef and then she was gone, vanishing beneath the blue mantle of the open sea.

Drops of sweat rolled down the boy's face as he stared at the spot where the turtle had submerged until a kingfish suddenly leapt through his line of sight and he felt the clammy wetness of a plastic bag wrapped around his ankles.

He picked up the plastic bag, shook it dry and jammed it into his pocket, afraid that the next high tide would carry it out to sea where the turtle might mistake it for a jellyfish and swallow it, and choke to death.

A loud sucking sound came from the sand gumming the boy's ankles as he pulled his feet free and ran up the beach, alarming a vast herd of curlews who took flight and circled above him, filling the bay with their cries of complaint.

The boy grabbed his fuel can and jogged back between the turtle's tracks to the sea, and waded out to where his boat lay moored in the shallows, shuffling his feet like his grandfather had taught him to while he scanned the sand a few metres ahead for any bumps which might be the hump eyes of hidden stingrays.

He quickly filled the engine's fuel tank and yanked the starter cord, and the motor coughed and spat, and the boy twisted the throttle to full, and the little boat's prow leapt clear of the water, its propeller whining and stitching a flaxen wake as he pushed the tiller a few degrees to port and aimed for the gap in the reef.

The boat buzzed out into the open sea and the breeze was deliciously cool on the boy's face. He thought about the leatherback turtle, now safely back in her ocean home, and he felt light headed, and elated, and fiercely proud.

A cormorant flew low and fast around the headland, mobbed by ravens, and the boy vowed to return to the bay as soon as he could, with wood and wire to protect the turtle's nest. And he would be on the beach the night her eggs hatched, to protect her hatchlings when they raced for the sea. He was sure his father would come with him, and maybe even a brother or two. And perhaps grandfather would find the strength to rise from his bed and come too, Inshallah, when he heard what his grandson had to say. When he told him that the turtles had returned.